LOVE'S GLORY
A Flag Day Story

By

Darlene Franklin

Book 3 in Holidays of the Heart

*Thou hast given a banner to them that fear thee,
that it may be displayed because of the truth. Selah.*
Psalm 60:4

Scripture taken from the HOLY BIBLE, NEW INTERNATIONAL VERSION®. NIV®. Copyright © 1973, 1978, 1984 by International Bible Society. Used by permission of Zondervan. All rights reserved.

All of the characters and events in this book are fictitious. Any resemblance to actual persons, living or dead, or to actual events is purely coincidental.

All rights reserved.
ISBN-10:1-944203-05-2
ISBN-13:978-1-944203-05-4

I chose Garan for the hero's name in *Love's Glory* because it is so similar to my son's name, Jaran. Jaran, you have grown into a man to make any mother proud, and your faith shines to those around you. I am proud to be your mother.

CHAPTER ONE

Cheers for the sailors that fought on the wave for it,
Cheers for the soldiers that always were brave for
it,
Tears for the men that went down to the grave for it,
Here comes the flag!
Arthur Macy

Abilene, Texas, May, 1919

Alfred, one of the new flying aces, was finally coming home from the war in Europe. Beth Smith waited at the edge of the airstrip with her friend Agnes Collins, Alfred's twin sister.

Compared to the crowd that welcomed home the doughboys after Armistice Day late last year, the waiting crowd was small. Only about twenty-five people peppered the air strip, prepared to greet Alfred and his best friend Smitty, both flying aces shot down over Germany toward the end of the war. She had never met either of them, but she shared in the Collins's excitement.

Beth and Agnes wore matching outfits of white shirtwaists tucked into blue serge skirts and red satin sashes across their shoulders to complete the patriotic colors. Mr. Collins held a flag aloft, a brisk wind making the thirteen stripes and forty-eight stars ripple like clouds crossing the sky.

Everyone trained their eyes on the sky, each hoping to be the first to catch sight of the Curtiss flying boat that had helped the United States bring home the victory and end the awful war.

A tiny black speck appeared in the sky, and Beth's hand flew to her mouth. The crowd hushed as they spotted the aeroplane and heard the buzz of an oversized hornet sailing through the sky.

"I see 'em!" Agnes's youngest brother's voice was filled with excitement and awe. Beth tipped her head back until she could make out two shapes inside the flying machine that looked so unlikely to stay in the sky. She feared flying as much as her childhood friend Garan had wanted to escape to the skies. He'd enlisted, then disappeared, presumed dead. Beth blinked back the tears that threatened to ruin this special day. When she opened her eyes again, the two heads appeared closer. Lifting her toddler into her arms, she waved at the skies. "Look at the aeroplane, Dottie."

With all the head gear on the two men in the aeroplane, no one could make out their features. A long scarf flew behind the neck of the man in front. The United States flag decorated the tail.

The aeroplane swooshed above the trees. The man in the back seat waved and shouted, his words unheard over the roar of the engine. They went higher and higher, making an arc until they hung upside down before soaring down to complete the circle.

Beth had barely regained her breath when the aeroplane pulled out of the loop and landed gently. Agnes and her family rushed forward to greet Alfred as he climbed down from the back seat. When Beth hung back to give them privacy, Agnes called her forward.

Beth turned to the older woman beside her. "Will you watch Dottie, keep her away from the planes?" At her nod, Beth headed to join the family.

As she walked across the tarmac, the pilot climbed out. Imposing at six feet tall, he looked like someone she should recognize. He looked like. . .but he couldn't be. . .

He whipped the goggles and hat off his head, as shocked to see her as she was to see him. "Guten morgen, Elsbeth Koch. I didn't expect to see you here."

Beth's knees trembled and she stopped walking, afraid her legs wouldn't carry her. Agnes rushed to her, but the pilot reached her first.

"Mein Schatzi, I didn't mean to frighten you so." The smile on Garan's face didn't quite reach his eyes, as blue as ever.

"You are. . .they said you were. . .dead." She took a deep breath as his very real, strong, arms steadied her. She straightened her back and stepped backward.

"I thought I was too, for a time. But the good God kept us alive and brought us home." He nodded to Alfred. "I sent word to my parents and will see them in a few days, after I look into work opportunities. They told me you moved, but I never expected to see you here.

Beth looked to one side, ashamed of the letters he'd sent, daily. Of her mother's pleas, "Elsbeth, why will you not at least write to him and explain what happened?"

Beth shook her head. "We have a lot to say to each other, but this isn't the time or place. In fact, here they call me—"

"You never told me you knew Smitty!" Agnes' flushed face reminded Beth of all the romantic dreams her friend had formed surrounding her brother's comrade-in-arms. "Are you feeling all right?"

"Just surprised," Beth said. "I never knew him as Smitty." She stopped, not caring to use his given name in case he, like her, had chosen to put his German background behind him.

"To her, I am simply Garan Schmidt. We grew up together in New Brandenburg, Texas—Old Glory, they call it now. We want to shout from the roof tops that we are proud to be Americans."

Garan's wide smile, perfect teeth, thick honey-colored hair, and cerulean blue eyes, made him the poster-child of German Americans. Beth's almost-white hair and pale gray eyes said the same for her, but she had anglicized her name.

As far as the Collinses knew, Beth came from one of the ranches scattered across the Texas

Panhandle, not from the highly German Old Glory, new name or not. Garan came to her rescue. "All will be explained in due time. Today is Alfred's day. Your hero has come home!"

Agnes ran back to her brother's side. Garan held up an arm and offered it to her. "Come, 'Beth,' let's welcome Alfred home." As they approached the group, he leaned close enough to whisper in her ear. "You can tell me your story when you return with me to Old Glory. Where you promised to be waiting for me when I got home."

CHAPTER TWO

The red and white and starry blue is freedom's shield and hope.
John Philip Sousa

Garan couldn't keep his eyes off of Elsbeth—Beth, as she called herself now. He had dreamed of her often, kept her image tucked into the pocket of his flight jacket. Each time he touched it, he begged for her forgiveness, and the Lord's, for the unforgiveable things he had done before he left for the war.

Now she stood in front of him, prettier than ever, her figure fuller, her face rosier, than even his wildest dreams had conjured over the years since he'd last seen her.

Alfred lifted his eyebrows in an unspoken question, and Garan nodded. They'd shared many secrets during the long nights and days in the German camps. How strange that had been, listening to soldiers speak in the language he had learned in the cradle, his native tongue one that Americans identified with the enemy.

As the group crossed the field to the waiting cars, he caught Elsbeth glancing at him. She blushed, the same deep rose that made her pale skin appeared burned. However, a shadow darkened her eyes, and she seemed remote even as they walked arm and arm.

What did he expect? Aside from one, single, cold, dismissive letter, she hadn't written to him, hadn't responded even as his pleas had grown stronger. America might have won the war, but he feared he had lost the woman he loved.

Bystanders remained at the side of the road, one a woman with a cluster of children playing around her. A curly-haired, towheaded toddler stood in contrast to the other children, all with hair a shade darker.

As they approached, the toddler broke away from the group. "Mama." She ran in that ridiculous pace of a child who has only recently gained the skill to walk—straight at Elsbeth.

Elsbeth let go of Garan's arm and swept the child up in her arms, turning away from him. But he didn't need words to tell the story. A toddler, walking, running, maybe fifteen months old? With that blond hair and blue eyes? Who called his Elsbeth "Mama?" He found his voice. "May I see her?"

Elsbeth turned slowly, but the child didn't hesitate. "Hi." Garan looked into eyes an exact match for the ones that stared at him in the mirror every morning.

"What is her name?" Garan's voice ground like the gravel under their feet.

"Dorothy," Elsbeth said. "Dottie Smith."

Dorothy. Of course. Elsbeth had always said she would name a daughter Dorothy, after the character in the book *The Wonderful Wizard of Oz.* Garan couldn't make himself ask the other questions.

"She's almost fourteen months old. She was born on January 25, 1918."

Nine months after the last time he'd seen Elsbeth.

Dottie Smith. It fit, Garan supposed, along with her new name. "Why didn't you tell me?" He whispered fiercely.

"Not here." She joined the woman with the children, whom he learned was her landlady. The children were named in passing, along with a wide smattering of friends and family. Try as hard as he might, Garan couldn't keep his eyes off Dottie, the girl who must be his daughter.

At the welcome home party, he couldn't find a private time or place to speak with Elsbeth. She left before dinner. Garan had to stay, as a guest of the family. He listened more than he talked, and by dint of a few carefully placed questions, he learned Elsbeth's story.

Beth "Smith" arrived in Abilene in June, 1917, seeking work. She and Agnes met at work at the Collinses's department store. Before long they became friends. Beth presented herself as a war widow. Her husband had died in a training accident—and she was pregnant.

The Collinses took Beth in as one of their own, and kept her employed after the birth of her daughter early in 1918. She never said much about her family, or about her husband's, and they guessed they were estranged.

No wonder she had fled. If she'd stayed, she would have faced disapproval and shame—unwed and pregnant, without the man responsible there to protect her. The more the jubilant family heaped praise on Garan, the more unworthy he felt.

Only Alfred guessed at his secret worries. When at last they let the boys head to the room they would share, Alfred peeked out the door to make sure no one was close before closing it. "I guess my sister can forget her dreams of capturing your heart, Smitty."

Garan's ears burned bright red—a reaction that had caused much razing among his fellow pilots, claiming his ears shone like radio beacons, leading them through the night skies without running lights. "There was never much chance of that, Alfred. I'm sure she's a great gal, but—"

"Your heart was engaged elsewhere. I hoped she could change your mind, but the Lord had other plans for you."

Garan stared at the starry night, wishing he could be in the air, where earth's problems seemed so far away and he felt closer to God. Not that he ever felt that close, even though he had begged for forgiveness over and over. Tonight that same sin came back to smack him in the face. One night of giving into the desires of the flesh had led to an unwed mother, a fatherless child. He closed his eyes. Elsbeth would have to listen this time.

Alfred took a chair next to the window, looking up at his friend. "Are you thinking what I think you're thinking?"

"Yes. Tomorrow. The next day at the latest. Before I return to Old Glory."

Alfred's laugh jarred Garan. "Something tells me it won't be that easy."

CHAPTER THREE

We take the stars from heaven, the red from our
mother country, separating it by white stripes,
thus showing that we have separated from her,
and the white stripes shall go down to posterity,
representing our liberty.
George Washington, attributed

Dottie must have sensed her mother's distress. She hadn't spent such a fussy night since her last teeth came in. Not that Beth minded—she doubted she would have slept much even if her daughter hadn't made a single peep.

At last, the girl slept peacefully for a few hours, long enough for Beth to consider what to do. After breakfast, they headed out to drop Dottie with the lady who cared for her during the day.

As soon as her foot hit the sidewalk, a car door opened on the street, and Garan's tall form unfolded from the front seat. "Elsbeth—"

"Beth," she corrected automatically.

"We have to talk."

He stood there, so solid, so determined, so *masculine*, all the things she'd admired and loved about him for so long. As soon as she had seen him yesterday, she'd known this battle was looming.

Her lips thinned. "I must get to work. Mr. Collins doesn't abide tardiness."

"It doesn't matter. You will not work there much longer."

The strength she had been seeking shot up her backbone. "I must. It is a good job, a safe place to work, with good pay."

When she tried to move around him, he blocked her, shifting them closer to a car waiting on the street. "Get in the car. We can get there more quickly." He took Dottie from her arms and opened the passenger door.

Beth stared at him. In the past, she had loved the way this man got around her, but not anymore.

Dottie turned her head, tears forming in the eyes so like her father's. "Mama." Her legs kicked, eager to return to the ground.

Garan held the child, as if he were used to settling fussy toddlers all the time. He'd plenty of experience, with his many nieces and nephews. "Shh, little one. Your papa won't let anything bad happen to you."

Beth's anger blazed, but his look dared her to disagree. "You cannot deny the truth. Get in the car, so you can take the child."

Uncertain if she was making the right decision, Beth slid in and clutched Dottie to her breast. When Garan sat behind the wheel, she said, "I must take

Dottie to Mrs. Edwards. She only lives a block away. And then I work at the Collinses' store." She gave directions.

When Garan took them to Mrs. Edwards' home, he alleviated Beth's first concern. If he had wanted to spend the day with Dottie, she'd miss a day at work rather than let Garan take off with their daughter.

Garan hugged Dottie and walked with Beth up the steps. Before she could say anything to the Mrs. Edwards, he led her back to the car.

Beth jumped in. "We have to hurry. I am supposed to begin work in seven minutes."

Garan glanced at his watch and shrugged. Two blocks later, he missed the turn for the store. As she sputtered, he continued driving toward downtown Abilene. "What are you doing?" she said.

"What I—what we—should have done two years ago. I am taking you to the county clerk's office to get a marriage license."

In her deepest heart, Beth had hidden a hope that Garan might find her, forgive her, and court her. She wanted nothing more than for him to marry her and create the family they were meant to have.

But she didn't expect to be dragged in front of the justice of the peace against her will. "You can't—we can't—I'm not dressed. . ." As soon as she said those words, she knew she had lost her argument.

"We are not the first couple to marry as soon as the war ended. Alfred tells me there are several stores that carry ready-to-wear dresses in the latest styles. I also wish to wear something other than my uniform." He glanced at her, and she look away. "I know you were unhappy when I enlisted."

"Yes." After all that had happened, that argument didn't matter anymore. A marriage license? A shopping spree? What next? "I suppose you have convinced a preacher to perform the ceremony?"

"Yes." He flashed a smile at her.

What else had he planned? She should say no. Shouldn't she?

They parked in front of the clerk's office. Before he opened his door, Garan turned to her, and she saw the uncertain, earnest young man she had loved since childhood. The ice around her heart cracked.

He took a deep breath. "I know this is not what we planned. I know I have sinned against you in ways I cannot begin to understand. But my love for you has never wavered. And we have a child—a child who should have her father as well as her mother. Please." Tears came into his eyes. "Even if you no longer love me, we once loved each other very much. Too much. God willing, we can love each other again. But at least we can be a family. Jah?"

If she said yes, now, could she ever say no again?

How could she say no?

"I will. Marry you. I will be your wife in name only. Until—if—our affections change."

He relaxed and led her inside. Their time in the office flew, with well wishes from the clerk who helped them. Next stop, the dress shop. "You can't come in here with me."

Garan's eyes narrowed, as if gauging whether she would run. "I can't see you in your dress. I know the tradition. But I tell you this. I want you to buy a white dress."

Her cheeks flared. They both knew she didn't deserve virginal white.

"In my eyes, you are pure, cleansed in the blood of Christ." He dug into his pocket. From a velvet pouch he withdrew a brooch, with a star cluster center, surrounded by blue and red stones. "I found this in London, and it made me think of you. Of the stars I see in your eyes. Of the red, like a rose in your beauty. And the blue, which is both the color of your eyes and now of the courage you have displayed while I have been gone. Please wear this for me."

She took the brooch and, pretending to examine it, wondered at him choosing it for her when she hadn't written to him for so long. Had he truly remained committed to her for all that time?

Garan opened the car door for her, then walked into the store with her. While the sales lady swept Beth away, he whispered with the manager before he disappeared out the door. When the manager appeared at her side a few seconds later, she was wreathed in smiles. "I understand we are shopping for a wedding dress."

The clerk clapped her hands together. "What a happy occasion! How wonderful to see one of our brave fly boys come home to true love."

"Follow me." The manager—Della, according to her name tag—swept Beth past beautiful evening dresses to dresses in bridal white. "He insisted we choose white. He said you might protest, since you are a fairly recent widow." She pointed to the wedding ring Beth had worn to perpetuate her fairy tale.

A few fancy dresses hung at the back of the store, and Della gushed. "You have such a lovely figure, I'm sure one of these dresses will fit you perfectly. Perhaps with a few alterations—"

"There's not time for alterations." Beth stopped in mid-stride. She would not, could not, dress like a princess in a fairy tale.

To the side, she saw a dress that just might work. "Let me try that one."

CHAPTER FOUR

Off with your hat, as the flag goes by!
And let the heart have its say;
you're man enough for a tear in your eye
that you will not wipe away.
Henry Cuyler Bunner

"This suit is dated," Alfred said. "Why don't you wear your uniform? Everyone loves a man in uniform."

"Not my Elsbeth. She never wanted me to go to war." She wanted to get married to raise a family together. But he'd followed his heart, too, enlisting to fight for his country, for freedom. And look what he'd left her with. He shook his head at his best friend. "Neither one of us cares about fashion." After he fastened his cuff links, he flicked his wrists and ran his finger between his neck and tie. Alfred was right—the suit was dated.

"Stop staring at yourself, or I'll think you're vain," Alfred said.

Garan blinked. Fussing with his appearance allowed him to escape his fears that Elsbeth would run away and miss the wedding. As much as he'd wanted to pace outside the dress shop and whisk her to the Collinses' house, he had asked Agnes and her mother to accompany her instead.

"And here they come."

Garan relaxed. The wedding might really happen. The bride was here, and the preacher should be here soon.

He peeked out the window. Agnes stepped out of the car first. Elsbeth came next, and she reached down for young Dottie. A smile crept onto his face. He wanted, hoped, needed their daughter at the wedding, but he'd feared Elsbeth would resist. Even if she wouldn't remember, she should bear witness to the day.

Alfred tapped his shoulder. "Don't you know it's bad luck to see your bride on your wedding day?"

"It's too late for that."

Alfred lured his attention away from the window by cracking the door open, holding it open long enough for them to hear feminine chatter and laughter as the women came in. A few minutes later, Mr. Collins climbed the stairs to Alfred's room.

"It won't be too long now. Alfred, would you give us a minute?" Mr. Collins rubbed his hands together.

Alfred raised his eyebrows, winked, and left the room. Garan paced back and forth, nervous about this unexpected face-to-face.

"Sit down." He pressed Garan onto the cot where Garan had slept and sat on Alfred's bed. He flicked on the overhead light, revealing all the crags and lines of the older man's face, suggesting wisdom.

His host sat opposite and leaned forward. "In the months we have come to know Elsbeth, she has become like a daughter to our family, so I am speaking as her father might, if he were here."

Garan doubted it Mr. Koch would be so kind.

"From everything Alfred has written about you, I know you are a man of honor and faith. He's written of your bravery, too. Everything a father could wish for his daughter, but—"

"Yes, sir." Garan stopped. What could he say without revealing more than he should?

"You grew up in the same town. You probably knew each other."

"Jah." Garan cleared his throat. Beth would want him to use proper English. "Yes, we have known each other all our lives."

"Did you know her husband?"

Heat crept up Garan's neck. What should he say? "He was not the man I thought he was." That much was true. If Garan had truly loved her, he would never have taken advantage of her in the way he had.

"And this wedding? Is it truly what both of you want? Will your families approve?" He leaned close. "As honored as we are to host this wedding, why not wait until you return to Old Glory?"

"It's complicated." Garan wanted them to face the inevitable questions as a couple. "Mostly, I am a man home from war, eager to spend time with the women he loves."

Standing, Mr. Collins clapped his hand on Garan's shoulder. "Mrs. Collins says Beth is of the same mind. And there is the doorbell. The pastor must be here."

Garan followed Mr. Collins downstairs to meet the pastor. Reverend Stewart was dressed as formally as the rest of the party, a clerical collar adorning a crisp black shirt. "I am pleased to make your acquaintance, Mr. Schmidt. And delighted that Mrs. Smith—" His eyebrows lifted a little at the similar names, and he chuckled. "—has found a husband for her and her young daughter. Before we continue, I have a question for you. Mrs. Smith is a believer, and the Bible says she must not be unequally yoked with an unbeliever. Are you a Christian, Mr. Schmidt? Have you asked Jesus to be your Savior?"

"I have." Garan felt no hesitation. Salvation—and forgiveness—had been his lifeline overseas.

"Then, we are ready to start. Is the bride ready?"

Agnes descended the stairs first, dressed in a dusty rose gown that was pretty enough, but Garan couldn't keep his eyes off of the little girl—his daughter. She took the steps one at a time, dribbling flower petals on the floor. When she reached the preacher, she stood next to Agnes.

When the bridal chorus started, Garan's eyes swept up the staircase again. *Elsbeth.* Although the dress was what he'd known she would choose, she still took his breath away. She had chosen a suit in an off-white ivory color that she might wear again. The jacket came with a white ermine collar, gleaming and glorious. A white-brimmed white felt hat, decorated with feathers and ribbons, sat like a crown atop of her pale gold hair. The suit emphasized her tiny waist, and the hem was just high enough to reveal her slender ankles and calves. She had pinned the brooch he had given her to the left breast pocket, over her heart.

Mr. Collins led Elsbeth to Garan's side, and the ceremony continued.

Reverend Stewart read the familiar words of the wedding ceremony from a small black book. When they exchanged vows, Garan's eyes watered, and Elsbeth answered with a tearful smile of her own. The words, so familiar, engraved on his heart more deeply than his army oath.

Before he had a chance to breathe again, Reverend Stewart said, "You may kiss the bride."

Garan looked into Elsbeth's eyes, seeking permission for a proper kiss. Blue streaked through her gray eyes, suggestive of a deeper emotion. The parson coughed, the gathered Collins family laughed, and Garan leaned forward for a kiss—and couldn't quite reach Elsbeth's face for the hat.

With a shy smile, she removed the hat, releasing a few tendrils down her back, and flung her arms around Garan's shoulders. He sought her lips in a kiss, full of promise and commitment, as applause broke out in the room.

CHAPTER FIVE

Every heart beats true
'Neath the Red, White, and Blue.

George Cohan

They had done it. Beth was now Mrs. Garan Schmidt. She didn't regret it, not for one tiny second. At least, not until the ceremony and celebration ended, and the two of them checked into the Grace Hotel, in the finest room available. Agnes was taking care of Dottie for the night, so they had privacy——more than they wanted.

A large double bed dominated the room, and Elsbeth felt the heat in her cheeks when she looked at it. Nothing like the green grass that had been their bed the time. . . An unfamiliar feeling tickled her, one that she stamped down. This was a marriage, in name only. *At least for now.*

Garan was looking at everything except the bed. Glancing at him, she wondered if the same thoughts passed through his mind. Finally he cleared his throat. "Alfred made the reservation. He didn't know. . ."

Beth shook her head as if it didn't matter. "The bed is sufficiently large. . ." No matter how big the bed, even if a table separated them, she wondered if. . .

The violence of the way he shook his head suggested similar doubts. "I spent the better part of two years sleeping anywhere I could lay my head. The rug will feel like a feather bed compared to some of my sleeping accommodations." He loosened the tie around his neck, as if he planned to undress in front of her. She should retire to the dressing room, but she couldn't take her eyes off her new husband. Although leaner and paler than the boy who had left for war, he looked better than ever.

When she realized she was staring, she grabbed her valise. "I will go into the other room to change." She stepped into the dressing room and reached into her bag. Her hand encountered an unexpected sheer silk material.

A note written in Agnes' handwriting read, "Please accept this as my gift to you. May you have the most romantic night possible." Multiple exclamation points followed.

"Oh, Agnes, you have no idea." To her relief, her sensible cotton gown and wrapper remained in the bag. She would be modestly covered when she climbed under the covers, although she doubted that she would get much sleep.

When she returned to the bedroom, Garan had also dressed for bed, an open Bible in his lap. When he looked up, he smiled broadly. "You were so very beautiful today. I didn't have a chance to tell you yet."

She looked at the floor. "You were handsome yourself. Even without your uniform."

That made him laugh. "We have a lot to overcome. But I would like to begin our marriage with time spent with God, in prayer, in His word." He patted the chair next to him.

"I agree."

He let loose with a relieved sigh. "I was afraid you would object, after the way I disrespected you—and God."

"I broke the same laws," Beth said. "All the more reason why we should start over the right way. After all." Her hand crept out of her lap, wanting to caress his chin, until she pulled it back. "Your name means 'guardian.' Mother told me once, when she said I could always trust you." She swallowed the rueful chuckle.

"When I was flying, I thought I was guarding our country. For the United States is our country. Even our town has changed its name, for those who questioned the allegiance of German-Americans." He shook his head. "That is an old argument, and this is not the time to bring it up."

His Bible lay open to the middle—the Psalms, Elsbeth knew without looking. She peeked, relieved to see he held his English Bible, not Luther's

German translation still used in their home church, as far as she knew. They might have changed by now.

"I have thought that our marriage must be based—on faith and love, yes, but also on trust and truth." He jabbed his finger on the page. "I read the sixtieth psalm several times during the War, because it is about a war. But in the middle of the battle, David said, 'Thou hast given a banner to them that fear thee, that it may be displayed because of the truth.' God's flag will be over our marriage 'because of the truth.'"

Beth nearly choked on his words. "Then we are lost before we start. I haven't told the truth since we. . .since I. . .discovered I was with child." Heat streaked into her cheeks.

Garan stared at her, not speaking.

"I cannot tell our families what happened. I will not. They believe I married as soon as I arrived in Abilene." She lifted her head defiantly.

Garan gritted his teeth. "On that night, I promised to love you and cherish you until the day I die. Although what we did was wrong." He swallowed. "I meant every word. I will pray that God will make it possible to share the truth. There are bound to be rumors, whatever you said."

She shuddered at the truth of his words. "You pray, Garan. I go to church, but I feel as though the sky is a steel curtain, separating me and God." Turning her back to him, she sat at the vanity table and unpinned her hair, releasing the long strands of gold down her back.

Turning her back didn't lessen her awareness of Garan's presence. Never had the simple act of brushing her hair felt so intimate.

CHAPTER SIX

You're a grand old flag,
You're a high flying flag
And forever in peace may you wave.
George Cohan

Did Elsbeth have any idea how the sight of her long
hair enticed Garan? He watched, asking God for
patience until the day their marriage became real.
No matter how rocky the start, the banner of their
marriage was love——his love, and God's.

After she had fallen asleep, Garan took the
fluffy pillow from the left side of the bed for his
spot on the floor. A silken bedspread had slid off his
bride, leaving only a sheet outlining her curves. He
sucked in his breath, turning his face away while he
pulled the bedspread onto the floor with him.

He made his bedroll, turned his back to Elsbeth
and looked out the window. The sky had been his
workplace during the war. Now he was back home,

looking at the same sky, America still the land of the free because of the sacrifice of so many young men. Had they fought the war to end all wars, or was that an illusion?

Whatever lay in America's future, Garan prayed for peace between him and Elsbeth, for a warm welcome from friends and family when they returned to Old Glory.

For a loving, peaceful future for his daughter. *His* child. He had held Dottie once. She had wiggled, anxious to get away from this stranger, which only heightened his guilt. But many fathers had returned from the war to children they had never seen, or those too young to remember. He and Elsbeth could still create the kind of family a child needed, with both father and mother—something so many children lost in the war.

Garan reached for his Bible and pulled out the envelope which held his only picture of Elsbeth. It had carried him through many long nights, but it faded to nothing compared to seeing her in person. Watching her brush her hair, one hundred long strokes, had nearly driven him mad. Even now, he would lay beside her, if only to run his fingers through her long blond strands. *O Lord of heaven, may it be so.*

Closing his eyes, he turned on his back and used the discipline he had developed during the war to sleep at any place, any time, when he had the opportunity. Otherwise, he wouldn't have slept a moment until the sun rose in the morning.

His internal clock awakened him with the sun. He checked the clock—it was just 6 a.m. During the night, he had turned, facing the bed where Elsbeth slept. Her features, softened in sleep, reminded him of the girl he had fallen in love with.

She stirred, stretching her long, pale arms over her head, her eyes opening in tiny slits. It took a few seconds for the setting to register, for the mask to come over her face. Before she could cry out, he handed her the wrap she had set on the chair by the door. "I'll go to the dressing room." Along the way, he grabbed his slacks and shirt from the chifforobe. "Do you want to sleep longer?"

She chuckled. "I doubt I will sleep another minute."

He allowed himself to smile. "Take a look at the menu. We'll enjoy room service."

Surprise crossed her face for a moment before she relaxed. "That sounds good."

When Garan reentered the room, Elsbeth was wearing a skirt and shirtwaist much like the ones she wore in Old Glory, with a shawl around her shoulders, sunshine from the window pouring over her shoulders. "Orange juice! And coffee. Biscuits and gravy. . . There are so many things."

He wouldn't mind German apple pancakes. Maybe Elsbeth would fix them next week. She was a good cook, almost as good as his mother. If she had been working in a store five and a half days for the past two years, she hadn't had much time to cook. Caring for a little one all by herself, she can't have had time for fun of any kind.

"We've had a single night, not a honeymoon," he said. "You deserve a month at the seaside. Since we can't do that, I can at least offer you everything on the menu before we leave. Order one of everything."

She raised her hands in a helpless gesture. "Wonderful! I couldn't decide."

The food cart brought enough to give everyone at their wedding a small plate of food, but they both enjoyed the different tastes. He hadn't had many good meals since he joined the army. Aside from enhanced womanly curves, Elsbeth appeared to have lost weight. The meal was good for both of them.

"I'm not sure I would want caviar again." He pushed the tiny plate away.

"Me either," Elsbeth said. "And I prefer bratwurst to that chorizo. But I would like the recipe for the soufflé." She kissed her fingers. "As good as a plain Frühstück is, I'd like to learn more about food from around the world." She smiled, but a hint of their old arguments about bringing New Brandenburg closer to American ways clung to her words.

He had fought and almost died for the grand old flag, and she still questioned him? He decided to tease her right back. "I would have to agree. After the pâtisseries I enjoyed in Paris, where lovely French mademoiselles served delicious pastries. . ."

Her eyes glittered. "You'd better be careful. You have your own frau now, as well as kinder. No more pastries served by mademoiselles for you."

He laughed. "There was never any chance of that. I only mean that if my frau cooks me French food, I will be happy to eat it."

"Good." She looked happy, as if this were an ordinary honeymoon. "I will have to buy a cookbook to try new recipes in our home." She set down her fork. "Where are we going to live? Do you know? What are we going to tell our parents?"

That depended. "What have you told people about Dottie? They *do* know. . ." His voice trailed away as she looked out the window.

Her cheeks pinked when she faced him. "I told them I married a soldier as soon as I arrived in Abilene, who died in a tragic accident. They think Dottie is a few weeks younger than she is. She was born two weeks late, so by now, the age difference isn't as obvious."

Elsbeth had lied about the child's father, a marriage, her birthday. How could they find their way back to the truth in her web of deceit?

"I didn't want to dishonor you, your family, your child." She lifted her chin proudly. "As it is, people will think me hasty to marry—as soon as you left. And now, as soon as you returned. You may be sorry you asked for my hand." In spite of her proud pose, tears glinted in her eyes.

"Never, mein Elsbeth. You always had and always will have my heart." He took her hand and pressed it against his chest, where she could feel his heart beating. "We will make our way."

CHAPTER SEVEN

Oh! say, does that star-spangled banner yet wave,
O'er the land of the free and the home of the brave.
Francis Scott Key

Beth put the troubling breakfast conversation
behind her when they returned to her apartment.
She hadn't allowed herself to dream of going home,
let alone as Garan's wife. She had built a good life
for herself in Abilene, and her familiar hometown
would now be different. The thoughts tossed around
in her mind while she packed her pitifully few
belongings. Dottie's things she had in abundance, as
if the perfect clothes and toys could make up for the
lack of a father and her long days at work.

While she packed, Garan attended to Dottie.
Every time Beth put a toy into a box, Dottie took it
out again.

Garan laughed at his daughter. "You will have
it again, when we get to Old Glory. Your

grandparents will have more toys for you to play with." He picked up a small carved train engine and rolled over the floor. "I had one just like this when I was a little boy. In fact, I got a new train car every year on my birthday, until every kind of car from engine to caboose."

"I want." Dottie reached for the engine and ran it along the rug, chugging with the sound of an engine.

"I remember that train. You put it around the Christmas tree when it got long enough. Your parents must still have it."

"My nephews played with it every time they came to visit." Garan had one older brother and two older sisters, unlike Beth, who was the oldest of her family.

Mother hadn't wanted her eldest to leave home two years ago. Would she welcome her back? Garan glanced at her, and she realized she had stopped packing while worrying about going home. If she didn't finish, they wouldn't leave on time.

Someone knocked at the door, and Garan opened the door to find the Collins family on the other side.

"We have a surprise for you." Agnes' grin suggested she desperately wanted to spill the secret. When she glanced at the window, Beth looked down at the street. One of the cars from the Collinses' car dealership sat on the street, behind their own family car. A Model T, the car Mr. Collins recommended as the best car for the price, especially for a family.

"You didn't." Beth motioned for Garan to join her, pointing to the car.

"We did." Mr. Collins stood behind them at the window. "It's not new, but it is in good condition. I have helped more than one of our boys get a car when they came home, and I can't think of anyone more deserving of this car than the man who saved my son on more than one occasion, and married a woman who is like my daughter." Mr. Collins extended his open hand and presented the car key. "Please accept this, with my thanks, on behalf of a grateful nation, on this happiest of occasions."

"Up." Dottie lifted her arms for Beth to pick her up. When she saw the car, she squealed.

"That settles it. Dottie likes it." Garan grinned and Dottie reached for him. She accepted him easily, the two of them already forming a bond. Beth should be delighted. Was she childish enough to wish Dottie would reject her father for not being at her birth?

Beth returned to packing the last few items into boxes. Old Glory looked forward to the return of Garan "Smitty" Schmidt, war hero. They didn't expect the prodigal daughter, who'd disappeared two years ago without warning. She hoped her presence didn't dampen Garan's welcome.

Before long, they were ready to go. How nice not to have to travel to Old Glory by bus. Someone—Alfred?—had tied tin cans to the back of the car, with a "just married" sign. Garan didn't seem to mind, so she didn't make a fuss. Before she knew what had happened, they were closed in the car and the Collinses were waving goodbye as

Garan pointed the car toward the road that would take them to Old Glory.

Once they had left the town behind, Garan pulled to the side of the road. "It will only take a few hours. It's only sixty or seventy miles." He jumped out and removed the tin cans. "I'll leave the sign." He grinned at Dottie, who'd scooted behind the wheel. "How do you like the car, young lady?"

"Whee!" Dottie said. "Go."

Garan's glance told Beth she might not like his next move. Instead of moving the girl, he held her in his lap when he sat behind the wheel. "Help me drive."

Keeping his hands firmly on top, he placed Dottie's hands on the wheels, controlling the motion while she waved her arms about like a bandleader. "Look, Mama."

Beth swallowed the scream rising in her throat, afraid of what would happen if Garan had to hit the brakes. They would fly forward the way a rider did when a horse stumbled, only with metal instead of horse's legs crushing their frail bodies. Instead of worrying, Garan explained different knobs and devices on the dashboard, and Dottie nodded as if she understood.

"You are a brave woman, Elsbeth. You faced an impossible situation and made a good life for you and our daughter. But. . ." Garan glanced at her again, his eyes aimed at her heart. "She needs a father, Elsbeth. Together, we can teach her to be true and brave."

CHAPTER EIGHT

Freedom's natal day is here.
Fire the guns and shout for freedom,
See the flag above unfurled!
Hail the stars and stripes forever,
Dearest flag in all the world.
Florence A. Bauer

The trip to Old Glory took longer than Garan had expected. At first, he drove slowly in order to become familiar with the car Mr. Collins had given them. With Dottie in his lap, he slowed his speed further, to allow for unforeseen accidents. He hadn't missed the fear in Elsbeth's eyes, although she didn't protest. She was indeed a brave woman.

More than that, she was the woman he had always loved, whom he didn't deserve, whom he had hurt and injured. He had prayed for the opportunity to ask forgiveness and to make restitution. Marriage could be that chance, or it could turn into prison for both of them.

These first few weeks at home would go a long way in testing their decision to marry. When they reached the city limit, he shoved his worries away. The next hour was crucial.

His eyes rested on the sign marking the entrance to the town. "Old Glory. I haven't seen the sign since they changed the name." Tears Garan hadn't expected formed in his eyes. He pulled to the side of the road. Dottie twisted the steering wheel, puzzled when the car didn't move.

Garan helped Elsbeth out of the car and walked to the sign. She touched the fresh paint on the sign. "Old Glory. Founded 1903. Population 200. We've come home to a place that's different from the one we left."

"They felt they had to do something to prove their patriotism. When I joined the army, I soon realized the truth of what you had told me all along. Other Americans didn't trust Americans of German descent. That's why I accepted the nickname 'Smitty.' It was easier for everyone."

Elsbeth put her arms around him, leaning her head on his shoulder. "I worried about you."

He put one arm around Elsbeth and another to pull Dottie into their circle. "You worried about me, in spite of everything?"

"Because of everything." She reached up and touched his cheek. "Why do you think I transformed myself to Beth Smith? So that our daughter wouldn't have to prove herself because her ancestors arrived in Indianola and headed for New Braunfels, not Plymouth Rock. You've heard about that horrible Hoodoo War in Mason County, all because of the fights between 'Germans' and 'Americans'"

"Both of them a murdering bunch." Garan muttered. New Brandenburg set out to prove they were different, even to the point of changing the town name. He envisioned the church now with a sign saying "Old Glory Church" instead of "Kirche in neue Brandenburg."

"The war changed us," Garan said, "but our families probably changed as well. The only One who has not changed is our Lord. He will help us find our way." Garan spoke with more assurance than he felt.

Elsbeth hugged him. "God does not change. Our lack of understanding—and even our doubts— don't change the truth."

He kissed the top of her head. "You are wise beyond your years, wife. Let's go home."

The three of them returned to the car, Garan and Elsbeth swinging Dottie by the hands between them. A quarter of an hour later, they made their way down the street where the Schmidts lived. Every house boasted a flag. At his house, bunting in the same three colors were draped across the porch. A large crowd spilled down the steps, across the lawn, and on the street.

A dog barked and ran towards the car, announcing their arrival. Shouts loud enough to be heard in Europe erupted as people surged forward. Garan braked as people swarmed the vehicle, arms reaching, kisses planted on his cheeks. Whispers rippled through the crowd, as more and more people saw who sat in the car with him.

"Let me through." The crowd parted as Mother approached.

Garan had sent a telegram. "Married Elsbeth." He didn't want her arrival to come as a total shock, but nothing could make the return easy.

Mother smiled at Garan but walked around to the passenger seat. "At last, I can you call you my daughter." The two women hugged as family long separated. Garan glanced through the crowd, surprised that the Kochs weren't present. Hadn't Mother informed them of the news?

Dottie reached to touch the woman hugging his mother. Garan hadn't mentioned the child in the telegram. Some news must be delivered in person. "This is my daughter, Dottie," Elsbeth said.

Garan's heart sank. He wanted to stand on top of the car and shout, "She's *our* daughter, Elsbeth's and mine." Apparently his wife wasn't ready for that announcement.

When he didn't say anything about Dottie, the joy dimmed in Elsbeth's eyes. He had failed her somehow. "I married a soldier shipping out as soon as I got to Abilene. He died in the first action he saw." She looked at Garan, defiantly, her lie now established as fact.

He could blame no one but himself. Forcing a smile on his face, he pulled her closer to himself. "When I saw Elsbeth in Abilene, I felt like God had given us both a second chance. I couldn't wait to bring my new family home." He waved his arms to include the crowd.

Once the awkward moment passed, everyone swarmed forward. Hugs abounded, and Dottie was passed from neighbor to neighbor. The familiar mixture of English and German surrounded them, enveloping him in the home of his childhood.

"Come here, come here. We have enough to feed an army." Liesel, Garan's sister, led them to a table groaning with food.

The outpouring of love should have pleased Garan, but he wished his homecoming were a quiet affair. A private welcome would have been easier on all of them. Liesel handed Dottie back to Elsbeth. "Let me get your plate."

"I'll do that," a familiar voice said. Mrs. Koch, Elsbeth's mother, had at last arrived.

CHAPTER NINE

*The flag of the United States has not been created
by rhetorical sentences in declarations of
independence and in bills of rights. It has been
created by the experience of a great people, and
nothing is written upon it that has not been
written by their life. It is the embodiment, not of a
sentiment, but of a history.*
Woodrow Wilson

Beth leaned against the car so she wouldn't fall.
With so many people crowding in, the sounds
sights, and smells, of the town she had left behind
overwhelmed her. The afternoon sun poured on her
head like warm oil.

Just when Beth had convinced herself her
family wouldn't come, her mother arrived. Before
she acknowledged her daughter's presence, she
hugged Garan. Beth's stomach twisted. What else
should she expect? She was the prodigal daughter,
the one who'd left suddenly and married hastily.

Even after she was left widowed and with a child, she'd refused to come home.

Why had Beth married Garan, knowing she would face their questions?

Mother let go of Garan and came to Beth. "This must be my granddaughter." When she reached out, Dottie buried her face in Beth's shoulder. "The poor child must be tired." Mother touched her head, brushing her granddaughter's hair away from her face. Leaning forward, Mother whispered in Beth's ear. "Do you want to stay with us for a few days?"

That one question was an olive branch, an acceptance, a hint of understanding, all in one, and more than Beth deserved. But, as much as she wanted to—

As if aware of her predicament, Garan appeared at her side. "Good news. Now that all of their children have married, they have two rooms we can use. They're excited about turning Liesel's old room into a nursery for Dottie."

Beth gave an internal sigh for the room she shared with her sister in her parents' home. "That does sound good. Mother just offered us a room—"

"I understand. Things are crowded at our house." Mother must have anticipated Beth's answer. "I brought a few things for you and for Dottie." Her eyes betrayed her hunger to hold the girl she had never seen before. "I will come back to visit another time, when there are fewer people around."

"Where is Father?"

Concern crossed her mother's face. "We will talk more later."

Beth handed Dottie to her mother for a quick hug and kiss. "This is your grandmother, Dottie." With a puzzled look, she pointed to Mrs. Schmidt. "She is your other grandmother."

Mother kissed Dottie and handed her back to Beth. "God bless you." Her mother faded into the crowd, taking a piece of Beth's heart with her.

Garan reappeared with their luggage. "See you later, Mrs. Koch." He put his arm around Beth and raised the other in a wave. The crowd, sensing he wanted to talk, quieted down. "Thank you for the warm welcome home. We've had a tiring few days. Please let us newlyweds have some time alone."

When he said the words, his skin turned red. His boyish touch charmed everyone, and people left in groups of twos and threes, laughing as they went.

Mrs. Schmidt asked Beth to call her "Anna," although the name stuck in her throat. Garan's family had assembled, three siblings with their families. Dottie soon forgot her shyness, running and shouting with the other children. The mixture of German and English didn't confuse her. Perhaps she would grow up speaking both languages easily.

The family begged for stories of Garan's exploits as a flying ace. So many details had been censored during the war. Beth heard enough to admire his bravery and patriotism, but the last few difficult days had taken their toll. She nodded once or twice before sleep overtook her.

"Sweetheart." A deep voice spoke in her ear, and Beth turned to find the familiar face, the lips she dreamed of kissing, before she remembered where she was. Garan slipped one arm behind her back and the other under her legs before she realized he intended to carry her.

"Garan." Her protest sounded scandalized.

"It is the tradition for the groom to carry his bride over the threshold of their home." Nodding his chin at his mother, he asked, "My old room?"

She shook her head. "The room your sisters shared. It's a little bigger, and next to the nursery."

Garan carried her as if she weighed no more than a feather, and she relaxed, trusting him to bring her to safety. Focusing on him helped her to ignore the titters from the people watching below. Somehow he opened the door and carried her to the bed. "You're hot." He unbuttoned the top button of her shirtwaist and, once he discovered she was wearing a camisole, he removed the outer garment. Beth wanted to protest but couldn't bring herself to it.

He lowered the blinds, but lifted the window, so that a faint breeze caressed her skin. "Rest well, my darling." As she drifted off to sleep, his lips brushed her forehead.

Beth didn't awake again until feet ran across the floor and Dottie bounced onto the bed. "Mama eat."

Garan followed, holding a tray with a steaming bowl of what smelled like Kartoffelsuppe, potato soup. "Dottie was worried that you would be hungry, so we brought you supper."

Keeping the sheet in place, Beth sat up in the bed. Although she wasn't hungry, they wouldn't leave her alone until she ate something. After the second bite, her stomach roared, ravenous, and she downed soup she hadn't eaten since she left home. "I had forgotten how good potato and cheese soup tasted." She dabbed her mouth with her napkin and patted the spot next to her. "Dottie, do you want to share my strudel?"

With an eager nod, Dottie jumped onto the bed. After Beth gave her a forkful, Dottie wanted to return the favor. Beth pointed to Garan, and Dottie liked the idea. By standing on the bed, she managed to get most of the strudel into her father's mouth. "Thank you." Garan swallowed. "I think."

Dottie laughed, and Beth joined in. They finished the plate in quick order, with Dottie chasing strips of pastry with stubby fingers.

"Do you want another piece?" Garan asked. "You weren't supposed to share it with us."

"Of course not." Beth felt full. "If I eat too much of your mother's food, I'll soon be a Kuh, a fat cow."

Garan's gaze swept the bed, where the sheet outlined her body. "I doubt that. You could use a little meat on your bones." He stroked her arm.

Dottie placed his hands over Garan's, pushing futilely. "My mama."

Garan looked at Beth, despair in his eyes.

"It will be okay. I promise."

"Will it?" He opened the closet and reached for an extra blanket. "I know who'll be sharing your bed tonight, and it won't be me."

As Dottie snuggled next to Beth in the bed, her warm body close to her heart like so many nights before, she told herself that was what she wanted.

Wasn't it? She had demanded the promise from Garan.

So why did she stare at his form, wishing his arms held her the way she held their child?

CHAPTER TEN

*I am whatever you make me, nothing more. I am
your belief in yourself, your dream of what a
people may become.... I am the clutch of an idea,
and the reasoned purpose of resolution. I am no
more than you believe me to be and I am all that
you believe I can be. I am whatever you make me,
nothing more.*
Franklin Knight Lane

Late that night, when Garan was certain Elsbeth
was asleep, he slipped under the covers on the far
side of the bed and lay as still as he could. He could
think of no other way to fool his parents into
thinking he had and Beth shared the marriage bed.

Before the sun arose, he slipped back out. If
Beth saw him in the bed, she might question his
willingness to wait, as he had promised. He ached
for his wife in the way God intended. For now, he
asked God for the right time. She wasn't ready. Not

like the young girl who had abandoned her principles for one night.

God had forgiven him. The Bible said so, even if he still felt guilty and ashamed. But forgiveness didn't wipe away the consequences of sin. If he spent the rest of his married life sleeping on the floor because of the way he had hurt Beth, he deserved no better.

Dottie cried out. Beth stirred, but before she came fully awake, Garan swept the girl out of the bed. "You're wet." He laid a towel on the floor and reached into the drawer for a dry nappy. As the youngest child, he didn't have much experience, but he would try.

If only Dottie wouldn't squirm and turn from side to side. As soon as Garan got one side pinned, she slipped away, crawling a few inches before standing, the diaper falling to her ankles. He was wrestling Dottie to the floor again when he heard giggling.

Elsbeth knelt on the floor next to them. "She's a wiggling worm all right." She tickled Dottie, and she laughed. Before she slipped away again, Elsbeth had pinned it on. "Quick and easy, that's the key. But thank you for trying."

Dottie pointed to a cup, and Garan handed it to her. As she drank the water, he wondered if Elsbeth had been able to nurse their baby, and for how long. He clenched his fists, angry at how much she had lost, at how much he had missed.

Their losses continued to mount. With their decision to forego normal relations between man and wife, would Dottie be their only child? Would he ever receive full redemption for his sin? Had Elsbeth asked for forgiveness? How could he ask, when he was the greater sinner?

Dottie touched his leg. He lifted her into his arms, hugging her close and kissing her cheek. Inordinately pleased that his daughter didn't resist his caress, he kissed the top of her head. "I love you, daughter." He set her on the floor and rolled a ball in her direction.

Elsbeth had draped her clothes over her arm, but she didn't seem in a hurry to get dressed. Instead, she waited, watching them playing together.

Dottie squealed when the ball rolled under the dresser.

"She's a happy child. You've done a good job with her."

Elsbeth's answering chuckle sounded strained. "I hope so. I prayed for Dottie so many times, before she was even born. She was conceived in sin, but she was innocent. I begged God to not let our choices give her a bad start. That is why I told the lies that I did. I felt that the truth would ruin her future." She swallowed. "Whatever happened before, or happens in the future between us, surely we both want the very best for our daughter.

Garan hesitated before he nodded. Of course he wanted the best for Dottie. But lying wasn't the best way to realize that goal. "Of course I agree with you about our daughter, but I'm not sure about your methods."

She crossed her arms, a shield against him.

He swallowed before he continued. "I have no right to criticize your choices. All we can do for now is find our way for the future."

She relaxed a fraction. "The future will be ours together, I promise. But I don't know where to start." She smiled at him shyly. "I never thought we would feel like strangers."

Garan answered with a wry smile. "Me neither. But we'll take it one day at a time." A thought jumped into his mind. "Has Dottie been christened?" Most babies were dedicated to the Lord within weeks after birth.

"No." The words tore from Elsbeth's throat, her eyes begging him to understand. "How could I promise to raise her in the faith without her father?"

Garan took a step back, his heart stabbed by the pain in her words. Before he could find the words to answer, she gathered her clothes again and ran into the nursery to dress.

CHAPTER ELEVEN

If anyone, then, asks me the meaning of our flag, I say to him - it means just what Concord and Lexington meant; what Bunker Hill meant; which was, in short, the rising up of a valiant young people against an old tyranny to establish the most momentous doctrine that the world had ever known - the right of men to their own selves and to their liberties.
Henry Ward Beecher

Garan's silence spoke volumes. Beth's fingers trembled as she tried to button her dress. Once she reached the top, she realized she had missed a hole and unbuttoned to the midpoint. After a few deep breaths, her hands steadied, and she completed dressing. Her hair fell in tangles around her shoulders; she pulled it into a loose bun. Her neck burned at the memory of Garan's attention when she'd brushed her hair the night after the wedding. Maybe he thought she hadn't noticed, but she was aware of him, as conscious of his every movement as she ever had been.

He knocked on the door.

"Come in," she said.

He smiled at her. "Mother's calling us to breakfast."

She touched her hair, tucking the loose strands into her bun. Garan stopped her hand. "You look good as you are. Come."

Heat tingled in her cheeks. She blushed as much as any bride.

Food filled the table, enough for the entire Schmidt clan. Her mother-in-law—Anna—smiled widely as they entered.

"Are you expecting company? Other than us?" Beth asked.

"Oh, no. I haven't learned to stop cooking for a large family, even now that my children are no longer home. And I don't know what Dottie likes."

"She's still eating soft foods," Beth said. Surely Anna didn't plan on giving her bits of sausage?

"I have plenty she can eat. Take a look."

Pancakes, latkes, apples, too. Eggs and bread. If Beth continued to eat at the Schmidt's table, she'd be a round frau in no time at all. "Anna, you must let me help you. Perhaps I can fix dinner."

"There is no need." Anna waved away her suggestion.

Mr. Schmidt laughed. "My Anna never lets anyone in her kitchen. I don't know how our Liesel learned how to cook."

"In my mother's kitchen." Beth smiled. How well she remembered the hours she and Garan's sister had spent together. "Then how else may I help?" Her mind skipped across household tasks. She needed to keep her hands and mind occupied.

"Nothing today, nor anytime soon. The two of you are still on your honeymoon. The little one can stay with me, if you want to spend time alone."

Heat rushed into Beth's face and neck at the same time Garan's ears flared red. He recovered first. "I need to find a job, Mother, to provide for my new family."

"You are welcome to stay here for as long as you wish."

No. Beth shuddered at the thought of remaining under her in-laws' roof longer than necessary. Garan put his arm around her, shielding her from his mother's good intentions. "But we can take a day or two together, jah, Elsbeth? You wish to visit your family."

Dottie was playing with her food. "Dottie will come with us today, after she gets a bath."

The nursery was a pleasant room. Dottie splashed in the water while it cooled down, sunlight pouring through the windows and keeping them both warm. Garan joined them, watching as if mesmerized by an ordinary bath. "She will be ready for a long nap." The temptation to postpone the trip to her parents presented itself, but she knew it was unwise. Her father's lack of welcome gave her no reason to stay away.

Garan picked up the outfit Beth had chosen for Dottie. "I like this dress, even if it suits a sailor." A wide sailor collar with a dark blue bow highlighted the white dress.

"They don't have a style for aeroplane pilots." Beth looked out the window. "How will you fly, now that the war is over?"

"Who says I want to?" Garan shrugged, but the expression on his face said differently. He wanted to fly, without question.

"You used to say air travel was the wave of the future. I'm sure you will have many opportunities."

"Until then." Garan waved his arm around their room. "We always have a home here." He sounded as uncomfortable with the situation as she felt. "Come, let's get going."

Beth looked at her image in the mirror, at the loose ends from her hair trailing down her neck. Her mother would say she looked like a mess. Tilting her chin, she tied a hat under her chin. The wind in the car would blow away apart any hair arrangement that required pins within the first mile.

In a few minutes they had settled in the car. Dottie climbed into Garan's lap without an invitation, her chubby hands grasping the wheel. "She loves cars as much as you did," Beth said.

Garan raised an eyebrow as he started down the street. "What do you mean?"

"Every time you saw a car, you'd run after it. You couldn't stop bragging when your father bought one of the first Model Ts."

"Ten years ago now. They felt like the best thing men could ever make, and that if we could cover the ground at thirty miles an hour and fly in the sky, we could do anything." His face hardened. "Instead, we killed each other by the thousands. Peace will only come when Jesus returns."

In that instant, Garan turned into someone Beth didn't recognize, someone who had seen death and horrors she couldn't imagine. Looking at the sky, he relaxed. "That's why I like the sky. Up so high, our problems seem so small and God seems so close." A grin split his face. "You'll have to come up there with me sometime."

"Oh, no." Beth leaned away.

At that moment, a bald eagle soared overhead, his loud cry the bell of freedom. What would be it be like to sit in the air, suspended between heaven and earth? Anything might seem possible.

Dottie pointed to the sky and extended her arms, flapping them like wings.

"Even Dottie agrees with me. Freedom flies in the skies. Try it with me."

CHAPTER TWELVE

You're the emblem of
The land I love.
The home of the free and the brave.
George M. Cohan

The sun climbed high in the sky, and Garan wasn't ready to go to the Koch farm yet. Mother had prepared lunch, so they wouldn't arrive at lunchtime, unannounced. Instead, he drove a short way to the Salt Fork Brazos River and found a spot that was quiet, cool from the noontime heat under a tree. He parked the car.

Elsbeth followed Dottie as she tottered through the tall grass toward the water while Garan retrieved the picnic basket. When he caught up with them, his daughter handed him a handful of black-eyed susans and bluebonnets. "Thank you. They're beautiful."

"They remind me of the flowers you used to pick me for me." Elsbeth picked a susan, tearing off one petal after another. "He loves, me, he loves me not—"

Garan clasped her fingers around the flower. "I love you, whatever the petals say." Elsbeth's lips glistened, inviting his kiss. He resisted, instead pointing to the picnic basket. "Let's head over to the trees and eat." Mother packed us a meal, so we could stay out for the day."

Elsbeth stayed next to Garan as they walked, their fingers brushing, and he wondered if he should have risked the kiss earlier, but the opportunity had passed. While they ate, Elsbeth kept a close eye on Dottie, who wanted to peek in the river. The food disappeared quickly, and Dottie climbed in her mother's lap. Garan leaned against the tree and held Elsbeth in his arms, and soon the three of them fell into a light sleep.

The sun had fallen past the zenith when he awoke, mosquitoes buzzing past his nose. Elsbeth had turned, her head pressed against his chest, Dottie cuddled between the two of them. The way it should be.

She opened her eyes, looking at him sleepily, her mouth so close. He leaned over, and she lifted her face.

Before their lips met in a kiss, Dottie stirred, and Elsbeth jumped up. "If we want to see my parents before dinner time, we need to leave now."

They had come so close. Garan wanted his wife badly, but he had given her his solemn promise. He should be glad she had pulled back, but he wasn't.

Instead of worrying about it, he cleaned up while Elsbeth tended to Dottie. The flowers she had given him lay crumpled on the ground, like so many dreams. "Let's go."

In the car, Elsbeth took an extra few moments with her hair. "You look fine. Beautiful," he said.

She stopped fidgeting, but a deep breath revealed her nervousness.

"You're worried about your parents," he said.

The glance she threw his way held daggers, whether fear or anger, he couldn't tell. "Not everyone is like your parents."

Garan thought about that. Mr. Koch had always been very straight-laced, old German, with little use for new-fangled American ways. He had remained steadfast in his opposition to America's entry into the war on the side of the Allies. "I'm almost surprised he didn't move when they changed the name of the town."

Elsbeth had a rueful laugh. "He ignores it. As far as I know, he still calls it New Brandenburg."

Garan needed to get something off his chest before they approached Elsbeth's family. "We should have married, two years ago. I know your father wanted to prohibit it, once I enlisted in the army, but I believe he would have come around. Especially when he met his granddaughter."

"What's done is done." Elsbeth shrugged. "We can only hope for a better future."

Garan glanced at the sky again, lifting an unspoken prayer for the coming confrontation. A few minutes later, they pulled up in front of half-timber house, a construction mixing wood and rock common to German communities. The well-maintained house with the perfect garden reflected the restrictions Beth had fled.

"I don't know what to say to Dottie. Father may refuse to even see us." Elsbeth trembled.

"I will not allow him to hurt you. You are my family." Garan's voice deepened and his back stiffened, his hands curling into fists.

"And you are not going solve the problem with fisticuffs." Elsbeth put her hand on the door handle.

"Wait. Let me help you."

She stayed in place until he opened the car door and helped her onto the well-manicured lawn. Garan put his arm around her shoulders while she held Dottie, keeping them both close and protected as they approached the house.

"Elsbeth!" A younger version of his wife, her next sister Gisela, ran out the door. "You came!"

Soon children circled them, three girls and two boys, from a teenager all the way down to a child who was still in diapers when he'd left Old Glory two years ago. The middle sister took Dottie in her arms. "Hello there. I am your Tante Hannelore."

At least someone in Elsbeth's family was glad to see her.

"Elsbeth. Schmidt." Mr. Koch's stern voice broke across the happy crowd and the children backed away, lining up against the house. Mrs. Koch came out the door, her eyes wide and hopeful.

Garan's grasp on Elsbeth's arm tightened as he walked them across the space to his father-in-law. "Mr. Koch, I thank God that we meet again."

The man harrumphed. "You married my daughter in spite of my objections." He addressed Elsbeth next, ignoring the child in her arms. "And you defied me, marrying as soon as you could find another soldier, and this—" He whipped his arms up and down indicating the child. "—leaving yourself with a child and alone. But I blame you." He pointed his finger back in his son-in-law's face.

Garan straightened his back. Mr. Koch might bring out a shotgun if they weren't already married.

"If you had married before you left for Europe, perhaps she would have at least stayed in New Brandenburg where she belonged," Mr. Koch said.

Garan swallowed. Her actions had avoided the embarrassment of an unwed pregnancy.

Mrs. Koch came down the steps. "That is enough." No one spoke as she joined her husband. "You are home now. That is all that matters. And our granddaughter." She held out her arms, and Dottie went willingly.

"Look, husband, she looks just like Elsbeth did when she was a baby."

Mr. Koch didn't quite smile, but he led them into the house.

CHAPTER THIRTEEN

*I swing before your eyes as a bright gleam of
color, a symbol of yourself, the pictured suggestion
of that big thing which makes this nation. My stars
and my stripes are your dream and your labors.
They are bright with cheer, brilliant with courage,
firm with faith, because you have made them so
out of your heart. For you are the makers of the
flag and it is well that you glory in the making.*
Henry Cabot Lodge

Home had changed since Beth had left, or perhaps
she had changed. Her youngest sister, Brigitte,
pulled Dottie into play. Beth's daughter followed
her with only a single glance over her shoulder. God
willing, "Tante" Brigitte and Dottie would become
close friends, along with Garan's nephew, who was
the same age.

Gisela followed Mother into the kitchen to
prepare food, but Hannelore crowded next to Beth.
When the boys diverted Father's attention, she

whispered, "Gisela is courting with the Mueller boy. She hopes Father will agree, now that you are home." Her eyes gleamed with mischief, and Beth remembered all the tales her little sister had spread about her courtship with Garan.

"Is that so?" Beth said.

"Is what so?" Father's attention turned back to her.

Beth didn't need to see Hannelore's finger to the lips to know to keep quiet. "How much everyone has grown. I hardly recognize Brigitte."

Father's face softened at the mention of his youngest child. "She will begin kindergarten this fall. She has grown too quickly."

"So we can be glad we have a new child in the family. Little Dottie is a sweetheart," Mother said. The two girls played dolls in the corner. Mother laid a tea tray with cookies on the coffee table. "I am so very glad to have you home again, as it should be."

No one spoke while they ate the cookies, as buttery and wonderful as Beth remembered. Father cleaned the crumbs from his mouth. "Garan, now that you are out of the army, how do you plan to support your family?"

Father had asked the same question two and a half years ago. He didn't like Garan's answer then, and he might not like it now.

"I believe air travel will become as important as cars in the future. I want to acquire an aeroplane as soon as possible, so I can get in on the ground floor."

Beth waited for the explosion, but Father simply shook his head. "You always had your head in the clouds, instead of grounded on the good earth God has given you to farm." He squared his shoulders. "I could use help. It wouldn't take long to put together a home for your new family."

Father's olive branch shocked Beth even more than Garan's plans to begin an aeroplane business. Her heart split in two. The offer cost her father pride and goodwill.

But Garan was no more a farmer than her father could fly. Smiles wreathed Mother's face, as if Father had offered the perfect solution.

Although Garan kept his face still, Beth sensed waves of panic. She decided to speak for them both. "We'll keep that in mind, Father. It's a very generous offer." She put her arm on Garan's arm, squeezing it in an effort to reassure him. "But I trust my husband's judgment about what is best for our future."

Father scowled, and the temporary good mood evaporated. Dottie starting fussing, tired, wanting Beth to hold her. Brigitte left the doll to dig through Dottie's bag. Beth looked at Garan, and he stood. "I appreciate the offer, Mr. Koch, more than you know, but we have a lot to consider." He took the baby bag away from Brigitte. "We will see you in church on Sunday, if not before."

With his trademark smile, Garan helped Beth out the door to the car. Tuckered out, Dottie curled up on Beth's lap and fell asleep, instead of demanding the steering wheel. They drove a few miles down the road before either one of them spoke.

"I am sorry for my father," Beth said.

"No. It is more than I expected. More than I deserved. It's just not—"

"You're not a farmer. I've known that for a long time."

"You know me well." He shook his head. "A piece of land like that would be perfect for a landing strip. But your father would see it as a waste of good farm land."

Beth wished she could deny it, but she knew better.

He glanced at Dottie, brushing the top of her head. "On a different matter, let's have Dottie christened now, since we are married. I am her father by law as well as by blood."

Beth settled back against the seat, her heart warring with his words. She hadn't trusted Dottie to anyone, striving to take care of her all on her own. Not even God got credit for the last two years. Beth felt she had done a good job.

"You're not ready." Garan's voice was rough. "We can talk about it again, later."

The list of things to discuss later grew longer daily. Her husband gave her more respect than she deserved. Garan "Smitty" Schmidt was her husband, a patriot, a war hero, one who had nearly died fighting in the war to make the world safe for democracy, in a land far away.

She might not be ready for everything he wanted, but she could make a start. Memorial Day was only two weeks away, but several families in Old Glory had lost sons in the war. They would honor their dead in private.

But the "Flag Day" holiday that President Woodrow had suggested, the day that the "stars and stripes" had been adopted as the official flag of the United States in 1777, was coming up in a month. That would give her plenty of time to plan a celebration honoring Garan and all the other soldiers who had returned home.

And maybe even the women who had worked and watched and waited.

Beth waited until Monday, when Garan went in search of business opportunities, to mention her idea to Anna. Her mother-in-law fell in love with the plan. Before the day was over, she had arranged for Beth to speak to the ladies' society on Wednesday.

A nervous Beth stood in front of women she had known since childhood, several close to her own age. The war had left two of them widows. What did she know of the price Old Glory had paid to support the United States?

With that in mind, Beth presented her idea, one that would honor both local boys and the members of Garan's flying squadron. The ladies agreed. All the soldiers would receive the welcome home they deserved.

CHAPTER FOURTEEN

When Freedom from her mountain height
Unfurled her standard to the air,
She tore the azure robe of night,
And set the stars of glory there.
Joseph Rodman Drake

Garan gathered with other members of the town on
Memorial Day, watching as one by one, wreaths
and flowers were placed on the graves added since
he had left town in 1917. He held himself together
as the brass band played "America," but tears he
couldn't contain fell when a bugler played taps. In
addition to the men lost in war, they had also lost
half a dozen men, women, and children to the
Spanish Influenza.

Why had God spared his small family, when so
many others died? All three of them had survived.
A blessing, undeserved, a sure sign of God's love—
and forgiveness.

A reminder that they still needed to make things right. Perhaps Elsbeth would be more receptive once he had settled how he would provide for them. He and Alfred had scraped together enough money to buy an aeroplane. Farmers would welcome an easier means to water their crops and apply pesticides. Oil men would welcome quick means to travel long distances. Local fairs would pay for air shows. People would flock to them for a chance to fly above the earth.

Their plans thought brought a grin to his heart, although he kept his expression solemn in honor of the occasion. The first person he wanted to fly with him was Elsbeth. Nothing made him sense God more than being suspended in the air.

The soldiers who had returned walked from gravestone to gravestone, planting flags next to markers and floral wreaths remembering their fallen comrades. After a final prayer by Reverend Bauer, the group sang "Amazing Grace" and "A Mighty Fortress is our God" before their dismissal.

The experience convinced Garan more than ever that he must continue his plans for the future, to honor the dead. The following Friday, he took Elsbeth back to Abilene while Mother kept Dottie at home.

"Why are we going?" Elsbeth asked for the third time.

"You'll see." His arched eyebrow teased out a smile from her.

When they reached the outskirts of town, Garan headed for route 29, for the strip where he had arrived only a month ago. Elsbeth twisted around. "This looks like. . ."

"We're not going to the house. Alfred's meeting us at our destination."

"It's a good thing I packed a lunch."

Once she saw his surprise, she might not want to eat. Elsbeth leaned out the window, twisting so she could see further ahead. "This is where you landed the aeroplane."

As if in answer to her unspoken question, a buzzing drone made itself heard above the engine noise, and Elsbeth looked up. "Did you bring me here to see another flight?"

Not speaking, Garan let the unfolding scene tell her the story. Alfred landed as they parked. To his surprise, Agnes had flown with him.

Agnes took the head gear off and shook out her hair. "Oh, Beth, it's wonderful. You're the luckiest girl in the world."

Elsbeth shook her head. "I can't believe you went up in that thing."

"It was the best time I've ever had." Agnes hardly stopped talking while they ate. Elsbeth listened, interested, intrigued, even. *Good.*

As they chatted, Garan compared the two women. Although Alfred had never said so, Garan suspected he hoped his friend would fall in love with his sister. Agnes was pretty enough to be on the stage, but who wanted a star when he had the sun and moon in Elsbeth?

No doubt Agnes was kind—look at the way the family had taken Elsbeth and Dottie in, no questions asked. She was a Christian, her faith strong. Unlike

Elsbeth, who looked like she was ready to bolt when communion started during the Sunday service.

For whatever reason, her reluctance made him love Elsbeth all the more. In spite of her struggles, she sought God in the midst of her pain.

When they finished eating, Garan showed off the aeroplane to Elsbeth from nose to tail and wing to wing. She asked questions about every nut and bolt and stretched her arms out at the same angle as the wings, shaking her head.

"People can't fly. So why can that contraption of wood and wires?"

Alfred laughed. "I don't understand the science. The Wright brothers did the most to make it work."

Garan ducked under the wing and opened the door to the cockpit. "I understand most of it, can even think of a few improvements. But as they say, bees shouldn't be able to fly. But they do. God made them that way."

Elsbeth laughed. "That doesn't help. God didn't make that flying machine." She held up a hand. "But I know you're going to say. God gave men the minds to invent it, the same way they invented a car. And cars don't scare me."

"Good. You're coming up in the sky with me, right now." With no further warning, he set in the seat, took the helmet and goggles that had been on Agnes' head, and adjusted them on Elsbeth. While she tucked her skirt around her legs, he buckled her in and studied her face. Panic flashed, but so did excitement.

"You'll be fine."

"What if I get sick?" Her voice rose as high as a little girl's.

"Use this." He handed her a paper sack kept for such emergencies, not that he expected any. After he buckled himself in, he glanced over his shoulder. "Enjoy the ride."

As he checked the systems and flipped switches, Elsbeth repeated the Lord's Prayer. After liftoff, he couldn't hear it anymore; or maybe she had stopped speaking.

Instead of the theatrical display he had used for his arrival in Abilene, he planned the smoothest of rides for Elsbeth. He climbed high enough to miss poles and trees but low enough for her to recognize familiar sights.

For him, the sky meant freedom from the earth's restraints, happier than he ever was on the ground.

He prayed Elsbeth would feel the same way.

CHAPTER FIFTEEN
I pledge allegiance to my Flag and the Republic for which it stands, one nation, indivisible, with liberty and justice for all.

Francis Bellamy

When the propellers whirred and the aeroplane raced down the road, Beth feared they'd never make it into the air. While the nose climbed, she wrapped her hands around her body. Not until Agnes and Alfred had shrunk to figures no bigger than squirrels below did she take her first conscious breath.

When they straightened out, Beth relaxed. So high in the sky, the farms, houses, and buildings below flashed by like doll houses. Garan pointed—conversation was impossible—and she saw a herd of mustangs running across the plains. The oil rigs that made autocars and aeroplanes work sprouted on the landscape. To think God had placed all that under the ground thousands of years ago.

When she spotted a flock of birds flying beside her, she smiled. The more she saw of the wonders of the sky, the wider her smile stretched. Soon, too soon, they descended to the ground.

When Garan unbuckled her, she threw herself into his arms and met his lips with a real, welcoming kiss, the kind a hero—a husband—deserved.

The kiss lasted until Alfred whistled, and Beth pulled away, embarrassed. Garan kissed her gently on the lips. "Don't worry. It's all right."

Putting a brave face on her embarrassment, Beth hugged Agnes. "You're right. That flight was absolutely amazing."

Alfred and Garan exchanged looks. "Then you'll be interested in our plans. Let's get some coffee in town and talk them over."

An aeroplane service, operating out of Old Glory? Beth loved the idea, but she wasn't sure it would work. She prayed it would, if God were listening. That ride in the sky made her feel like she could reach God for the first time in a long time.

Maybe He had reached for her, and she had rejected Him. She sent a prayer heavenward. *Please, God, don't let Your anger at me keep Garan's dreams from coming true.*

How could Garan grin as if he didn't have a care in the world? They had both sinned, both deserving of God's discipline. If she asked him, she knew what he would say. *God's forgiven me. He's forgiven you. Believe it.*

Garan hadn't spent two years terrified someone would discover their secret. Instead, as soon as he knew the truth, he had fixed it. He was as noble as Joseph, who'd married the pregnant Mary, and their marriage was as chaste as the biblical couple's.

If Garan could be noble like Joseph, why did she feel like Bathsheba? David made peace with God for what happened with Bathsheba. The Bible didn't say if she made peace with God, too. She must have done something right. God chose her son Solomon to be Israel's next king.

At church on Sunday, the congregation greeted the celebration of the following Saturday's Flag Day with enthusiasm. The ladies of the congregation buzzed and fluttered when Mrs. Bauer, the pastor's wife, sought her out after the service. "I hear this plan was your idea, Mrs. Schmidt. We are so glad to have both of you back with us."

Beth stammered thank you. Women around her embraced her and admired Dottie, not one questionable look. What would it take to feel like she belonged, again—in her town, in her family, in her husband's bed?

The question continued to bother her as they drove home. The verse Garan had shared with her the morning after their wedding came to mind. She looked for it in her Bible, where she had marked it, Psalm 60:4. "Thou hast given a banner to them that fear thee, that it may be displayed because of the truth. Selah."

The truth. Was the answer as simple as that? Did she have the courage?

The difficulty of the second question complicated the simplicity of the first. How?

Where? When? Preparations for Saturday's Flag Day ceremony hindered her from finding her answer.

Garan split the week between Abilene and Old Glory, hurrying to be ready for his surprise at the celebration. Anna, Mother and Mrs. Bauer spent every spare minute, with other ladies, working on the gigantic flag. Several times she wanted to ask about christening Dottie. Both grandmothers would be as happy as if they had been there for her birth, but she wasn't ready. Not yet.

Father had agreed for the community to hold the ceremony in his fallow field, the spot where Garan and Beth could build a house if they agreed to farm. Cars and wagons filled every spare space until she wondered if enough space remained for the day's events.

Attendance exceeded Beth's wildest expectations, more than the entire population of Old Glory. Almost all of the town folk came, joined by lots of the people from neighboring towns and families and friends from the flying squadrons in the area. No one could see the two aeroplanes hidden behind a stand of trees. The pilots would slip away when the time came.

The school principal had jumped into the celebration with great enthusiasm. He promised several interesting twists, and Beth waited with anticipation. The day began with the band marching across the field. They played a march that Beth recognized as "The Stars and Stripes Forever," one that was about as old as she was but remained popular. When they reached the crowd, another group joined the band, and they began to sing. Beth hadn't known Sousa had written words to a march. "Sing out for liberty and light, Sing out for freedom and the right, Sing out for Union and its might, O patriotic sons."

Beth already had tears in her eyes, and the day had hardly started.

The band leader stepped aside and the principal stood in front of the crowd. "Before we sing the national anthem together, our students will repeat a pledge that we began using in 1917, when President Wilson told us we should honor the flag. It was written by a minister named Francis Bellamy, who encouraged schools across the country to fly the flag in front of the schools."

Almost all the school children scrambled forward. The band leader raised the flag high in the sky as the children lifted their right arms in a straight-armed salute. Together, they said, "I pledge allegiance to my flag and to the Republic for which it stands, one nation, indivisible, with liberty and justice for all."

The principal turned to the crowd. "Would you like to repeat it with us?" He led them through, line by line. When he ended, a load huzzah went up from the crowd.

CHAPTER SIXTEEN

I swing before your eyes as a bright gleam of color, a symbol of yourself, the pictured suggestion of that big thing which makes this nation. My stars and my stripes are your dream and your labors. They are bright with cheer, brilliant with courage, firm with faith, because you have made them so out of your heart. For you are the makers of the flag and it is well that you glory in the making.
Franklin Knight Lane

Garan wondered how long the school portion would go on. Elsbeth had promised they would end with singing "The Star Spangled Banner," so he relaxed to enjoy what promised to be an enjoyable day.

After the pledge, the children rearranged, grade by grade. Elsbeth's sister Hannelore came to the front to read an essay explaining the symbolism of the flag. She reminded everyone that the flag contained one star for each state. The last two states, Arizona and New Mexico, had been added in

1912, bringing the total for forty-eight. "If you know the states, say them with us." With a curtsey, she returned to her spot with the other seventh graders.

The first graders started. "Alabama, Arizona, Arkansas, California." Each group repeated four states until the seniors got to the four W's, Washington, West Virginia, Wisconsin, and Wyoming. Garan looked at the Texas state flag, waving proudly next to the national flag, and remembered its status as once being a nation on its own. Then they came to their senses and joined the greatest nation on earth.

The children dispersed to their families, and the chorale re-formed to sing "It's a Grand Old Flag" from George M. Cohan's musical, "Yankee Doodle Dandy." At a sign from Beth, Garan and Alfred escaped to their hidden planes.

A lot was riding on his father-in-law's response to their demonstration. *Lord, let it be so.*

Garan and Alfred strapped in and prepared to fly as the final words faded away. At a signal from Alfred, they ran the aeroplanes straight ahead on a track behind the band separated by a rope with a "do not cross" sign.

As the aeroplanes roared down the field, gaining the necessary speed to lift off, cheers erupted from the crowd, drowned by the engines when the aeroplanes left the earth in unison.

The two friends gave each other a thumbs up before they flew in opposite directions. They flew apart, they flew close, almost nose to nose. They flew high, they flew low. This brought Garan such joy, flying high above the earth, lost in the air with no purpose other than entertain and celebrate freedom that the America flag represented.

Elsbeth needed the air show to last twenty to twenty-five minutes. About the time they began to make pictures with tail smoke, he caught sight of what was happening on the ground. A line of women held on to the upper edge of a flag, while a line of men unfurled it. He counted ten stripes so far. It looked big, perhaps as large as both sides of a sloped roof, almost big enough to count each individual star from the sky. Garan had known the ladies of the community had been involved in a large project, but he had never guessed anything like this.

He wanted to let the folks on the ground know his appreciation. No air maneuvers could create a flag. Maybe he could a write USA?

Alfred flew away to give Garan enough room for a single plane performance. Instead of the star he intended, he dipped the nose down and up in a loop, created the U. The slithering movements of the S were harder to manage, and the A looked more like an inverted V. He could only hope the people below understood the message.

By the time they finished their routine, the flag was unfurled. Alfred landed first, taxiing away from the runway so Garan could follow. Even before he turned off the motor, the crowd's jubilation was evident on their face. Today's celebration had outdone Memorial Day and the upcoming Fourth of July put together.

When Garan dismounted, Elsbeth ran across the grass, Dottie in her arms, and kissed him on the mouth. Her eyes danced with delight. "The truth will make us free, Garan. God used that song from Yankee Doodle Dandy to get through to me. 'Every heart beats true 'neath the red, white and blue.' Only the truth will set us free, the truth of Jesus, and the truth of what we did."

"Do you mean it?" He held her face between his hands. Before people crowded in, he said, "Then we will find a way to tell the truth. Soon."

The next wave included his family as well as the Kochs. His father-in-law took Garan's hand in a firm grip. "You are a fine pilot. A better pilot than a farmer."

"I'm glad you agree. We would like to accept your offer to live on your land—if you will allow us to build an airstrip for our business."

When Mr. Koch nodded before shaking hands again, Garan knew his dreams for the day had come true.

#

Sunday, June 22, 1919

With the decision made to tell the truth, the opportunity presented itself quickly. Beth and Garan had a long conversation with Reverend Bauer in preparation for Dottie's christening, and he agreed to their plan.

The extra-long christening gown which had seen all six Koch children dedicated to the Lord fit on Dottie as she toddled around, though it dangled a couple of inches above the ground instead of tucked beneath her feet. Beth hoped Mother didn't regret her gift of the gown after Garan and Beth shared their story in front of the church and community.

Today held another special celebration. Tonight, after they had confessed their sin publicly, Beth and Garan would consummate their marriage. The pull between them strengthened with each passing day. Noticing how his muscled form filling his suit and the way the blue of the jacket brought out the endless skies in his eyes, she imagined the fervent kisses they would share.

Because she thought it would please Garan, Beth wore her wedding suit with a rose colored shirtwaist to offset the creamy white of the material.

After the Flag Day celebration, Garan's popularity had doubled. Every person in town wanted a ride, and business was off to a promising start. All of them had crowded into church for Dottie's christening.

After the hymns, Reverend Bauer called them forward. Eyes twinkling, he whispered, "Courage, my children. Remember that God's banner is truth."

He took Dottie in his arms, and she squirmed, reaching for Elsbeth. "Mama." Laughter swept the congregation.

"Don't worry," she said. "Mama and Papa are right here."

Reverend Bauer raised his voice. "Today we gather together to dedicate this child, Dorothy Alice Schmidt, to be raised in the fear and admonition of the Lord. Today we will change the order slightly and begin with the church's responsibility. Please stand with me."

The beauty of the words struck Beth as never before. The congregation promised to recognize Dottie as a gift from God. To make every reasonable effort to build the Word of God into Dottie. To provide for her needs. To pray for her salvation. To recommit themselves as parents to their children.

Reverend Bauer repeated the promises with the grandparents, Mr. and Mrs. Koch and Mr. and Mrs. Schmidt. Alfred and Agnes Collins, the designated godparents, looked pale and serious as they repeated their vows.

At last the pastor turned to Garan and Beth. "Now we come to the parents. Elsbeth Koch waited to present her daughter to the Lord until her father could participate."

He placed Dottie in Garan's arm and placed a hand on each of their heads. "You see, in January 1918, Garan Schmidt was in Europe fighting a war to protect our country, the war we hope will end all wars. He was unaware that Elsbeth was giving birth to his daughter in Abilene."

Gasps erupted across the room, and the grandparents paled as they learned the truth for the first time. "Garan and Elsbeth, you have both sought forgiveness for your sins and I for one will not condemn what God has forgiven. You have obeyed God in joining in marriage to provide a home for your child. Do you now promise to recognize Dottie as a gift from God?"

When Beth looked at Garan, all the commotion faded into the background. Together they said, "We do."

After more commitments, when the ceremony ended, Reverend Bauer said, "Now it is time for the people of Old Glory to demonstrate the grace of God and their faithfulness to the promises they made, to God and in the presence of these witnesses, to assist Garan and Elsbeth in raising Dottie to be a child of God. Go in peace."

Silence greeted them as Garan led Beth and Dottie past the first row. In the second row, Gisela stood. In the third row, Garan's brother and sister-in-law stood. Across the congregation, several friends stood. Both sets of parents stood at the same time. Mrs. Bauer's voice rose in song, "To God Be the Glory." By the time they the back door, the congregation was singing the chorus.

"And give Him the glory, great things He has done."

Grace and truth, love's glory flew over Garan and Elsbeth's family in a banner designed by God Himself.

ABOUT THE AUTHOR

Best-selling author Darlene Franklin's greatest claim to fame is that she writes full-time from a nursing home. She lives in Oklahoma, near her son and his family, and continues her interests in playing the piano and singing, books, good fellowship, and reality TV in addition to writing. She is an active member of Oklahoma City Christian Fiction Writers, American Christian Fiction Writers, and the Christian Authors Network. She has written over fifty books and more than 250 devotionals. Her historical fiction ranges from the Revolutionary War to World War II, from Wyoming to Vermont.

Darlene Franklin
Writing at the Crossroads of Love and Grace
Latest release: *Beginnings: 30 Days in Genesis - Exodus; Tobogganing for Two*
http://darlenefranklinwrites.com/

The Reformed Cowboy in *The Cowboy's Bride Collection,* Barbour, 2016

A Bride's Rogue in Roma, Texas, in Brides of the Old West, June 1, 2015

The Face of Mary in *A Texas Christmas,* September 1, 2015

DRESSED FOR DEATH SERIES
Gunfight at Grace Gulch
A String of Murders
Paint Me a Murder

MAPLE NOTCH SAGA
<u>Maple Notch Brides</u>
Prodigal Patriot
Bridge to Love
Love's Raid
<u>Maple Notch Dreams</u>
Hidden Dreams
Golden Dreams
Homefront Dreams
<u>Maple Notch Days</u>
Saving Felicity
Small-Town Bachelor

Miss Bliss and the Bear in *Preacher Brides*
Priceless Pearl in *Homestead Brides*

COLORADO MELODIES SERIES
Romanian Rhapsodies
Plainsong
Knight Music
Colorado Melodies

Love's Raid in *New England Romance Collection*

It Is Well With my Soul

Calico Brides

Angel in Disguise in *Texas Brides*

Merry Christmas, With Love in *Postmark: Christmas*

A Bride's Rogue in Roma, Texas

Pride's Fall

TEXAS TRAILS SERIES
Lone Star Trail

First Christmas in *Christmas at Barncastle Inn*

Face of Mary in *A Woodland Christmas*

Beacon of Love

Seaside Romance

A READER'S JOURNEY SERIES
A Reader's Journey through Matthew

HOLIDAYS OF THE HEART SERIES
Christmas Visitors,
My Candy Valentine
Love's Glory

An Apple for Christmas

Made in the USA
Charleston, SC
26 February 2016